Have A Holly Jolly Shiftmas

A Smutacular Witchy Shifter Novella

S. P. Icey

Snow Pire Books, LLC

Published by Snow Pire Books, LLC

EST. 2024

Formatting by S. P. Icey

Proofreading by @maraeditiorialservices on Instagram

EPUB ISBN

PAPERBACK ISBN

First Edition December 2024

Dedication

For those who have entered their shifter romance era.

This one's for you.

Content Warnings

Violence, blood and gore.

On page sexual scenes.

BDSM, characters being tied up during adult acts.

Teasing, edging and foreplay.

Cussing and vulgar language.

Cliffhangers.

Have A Holly Jolly Shiftmas Playlist

Hey Daddy (Daddy's Home) (feat. Plies) by USHER, Plies
Fantasy by Mariah Carey
What's My Name by Rihanna
Are You That Somebody by Aaliyah
Rock Your Body by Justin Timberlake
Miss Independent by Ne-Yo
WAP by Cardi B
Like a Boy by Ciara
Unfoolish by Aaliyah
Check It Out by will.i.am, Nicki Minaj
We Ride by Rihanna
Love, Sex Magic by Ciara, Justin Timberlake
Damaged by Danity Kane

Touch My Body by Mariah Carey

Put It Down by Brandy, Chris Brown

Pon de Replay by Rihanna

Soldier (feat. T.I. & Lil'Wayne) by Destiny's Child, T.I., Lil Wayne

Show Stopper by Danity Kane

Driving Home for Christmas by Cristian Fenn

Holly Jolly Christmas by Michael Bublé

Maeli

I gasped and my mouth dropped to the ground in admiration. "Holy fuck. He's Huge!" My dumbbell slipped from my grip and narrowly missed the tip of my foot. I cursed under my breath.

My best friend, on the other hand, busted out laughing.

I stuck my tongue out at her. "I'm *so* glad you think me almost smashing the hell out of my toe is hilarious Kali."

Kali snorted as she gathered herself. "Maeli, you would've been fine and you know it! You'd just whip it back to normal in no time. Abra-ka-fix and blamo! A brand new un-broken foot."

I smacked her on the arm. "Keep it down! You know how these people feel about magic! I don't need anyone else finding out my dirty little secret." Last time word got out about someone who possessed a sliver of magic...half the town was burned down due to a literal witch hunt.

And the witch in question...was my biological mother.

Before you ask, no the townspeople didn't burn the place. She did.

Her little snake of a familiar apparently overheard a few humans gossiping about a witch sighting—a guy had claimed he'd seen someone flying in the night sky on a broom. Low and behold, it was my mother. The humans made their own—accurate—assumptions and showed up at her little home of gloom on the edge of town angry and asked her to leave town. No pitchforks involved. Just angry fist-waving humans.

She didn't take that too well.

The man who'd seen her broom and all was at the fore-front. She turned him into a toad and stomped on him until he was nothing more than a smear on the gravel beneath her feet. The townsfolk—understandably—didn't take that very well and ran away screaming. The moment they were off her property, the fires started.

Spiteful, that one.

I sighed. "Anyway, we need to finish up so I can bolt out of here on the off chance tall, dark, and gorgeous heard me. I don't feel like embarrassing myself." The individual in question was massive. Muscles covered every visible inch of his body. His thighs were thick and defined. His bulging biceps would put Thor's to shame. His onyx hair was braided down his back and fell perfectly between his lats. I was salivating.

Kali snapped her fingers. "Hello, earth to Maeli?"

Heat rose to my cheeks. "What?"

"If you're trying to avoid embarrassing yourself...you're doing a piss poor job of it," she snickered.

"Yeah well..you're not helping, you jerk." I huffed.

Kali not so subtly turned her head toward the muscle-man; a smirk blatantly plastered across her face. And in that moment, guess who made direct eye contact with Kali via the floor to ceiling mirrors that lined every inch of the gym?

Yeap. You guessed it.

The Muscle Daddy I was ogling.

Oh no.

Kali took that as the perfect time to full body wave at the guy.

Kali, you traitor. I'm hexing your ass.

This is it. I'm going to die of embarrassment.

He re-racked his squat bar—which held a hefty 870lbs—before he crossed the crowded gym floor to where we stood.

Fuck fuck fuck.

"Hello ladies, how can I help you?" The thick velvet of his voice sent shivers down my spine. My magic rippled in the base of my stomach, as if licking its lips.

"I...uh," I stammered, my mouth suddenly parched.

"I'm Kali and this is my friend Maeli. We were wondering if you could maybe spot her next set by chance?" Kali batted her ridiculously long lashes up at the man in front of us. Heat rushed to the apples of my cheeks.

"Actually, I think—"

The edge of his mouth curled into a smirk. "It'd be my pleasure. Maeli, was it?"

Kali giggled next to me. "Oh the pleasure is all hers...what was your name?"

He bent forward and slipped my hand on top of his before he brought it to his lips. His lips gently skirted across my fingertips. "You can call me Alastor," he purred.

My core melted. Every inch of my body—of my magic—cooed.

Okay. What is going on?

And why is this beautiful specimen of a man having this effect on me?

"Shall we?"

CHAPTER TWO

Maeli

*O*kay, *dumbbell press might not have been the best idea.*

Alastor stood directly behind where my head rested on the bench and spotted me as I struggled to lift my final set. My face was flushed from the repeated movement, or from the fact that my gaze continued to latch onto his compressed bulge, who knew.

Don't lie to yourself.

You're redder than a damn tomato because of the sexy package that's just out of reach.

I squeezed my eyes shut, trying to concentrate as my arms were halfway through the movement. I sucked in another breath before I released it, hoping that the rush of air would encourage my muscles to cooperate.

Thick heat whispered mere inches above my head, "Push, finish strong, Enchantress."

I abruptly dropped my weights. The hard rubber bluntly hit my arms before the weights collided with the mat below. I swore at the pain.

He quickly helped me up. His fingers gently grazed my soon-to-be-bruised skin. "Are you okay?"

"Yeah, just, uh, lost my focus I guess."

The molten amber of his eyes searched the stunned depths of my muted hazel ones.

Wow, even his eyes are gorgeous.

The corners of his eyes slightly crinkled as he smiled. "It happens to the best of us."

Alastor handed me a water bottle from beneath the bench,crouched in front of me, and placed his elbows on his knees.

"That's not mine." I shook my head.

"I know, I grabbed it from my bag."

I furrowed my brows, not remembering if he brought his bag or anything else over before he spotted me.

"You know, it's not safe for a woman to accept a drink from a stranger. How do I know you didn't tamper with it or something?"

He cocked a brow at me. "For one, the seal is still fully intact, I promise you. Secondly...based on the level of training you're doing—and I have no doubt that you could easily lift more than you just were—I'd be a complete moron. You'd undoubtedly kick my ass." He smirked.

My face heated. "How do you know I wasn't going for a personal record? And...you'd be surprised there's a ton of creeps out there."

He chuckled. "I saw you and your friend—Kali, was it? You were moving much heavier weight when I checked in at the desk." He set the bottle next to me on the padded bench and stood. "As for the creeps out there...I'm well aware. Dealing with them is a part of what I do."

I sent out a small tendril of my magic to search for Kali...only to find she left.

Best Friend my ass.

"This was my last movement. My arms were shot," I mumbled as I snatched the water he sat next to me and gulped it down.

"I have no doubt about that, Maeli." The dull overhead lights twinkled at the edge of his pupils.

"Why did you call me Enchantress?" The question leaped from my mouth way too loudly which caught the attention of a few of the gym bros flexing in front of the mirrors nearby.

Fucking hell, Maeli.

Could you have said that any louder?

Alastor smirked, clearly finding my outburst hilarious. "Well, isn't it obvious?" My pulse quickened.

Does he know?

Oh Gods, he knows. He's going to rat me out.

I'm going to have to leave town.

His smirk grew to a breathtaking grin. "I find you enchanting, Maeli."

I choked. "You what?"

Chapter Three

Alastor

Maeli.

The moment I entered the small run of the mill gym, she caught my attention. Her bubbly, warm laughter bounced off of the mirrored walls that lined a majority of the lifting area and dug its claws into my chest. I focused on the beautiful sound as I headed to the locker room, changed out of my uniform and into my grey sweats and tank. I shoved my clothing into my gym bag and followed the sound of the woman's succulent voice.

My breath caught when I laid eyes on her through the mirror ahead of the squat rack I'd chosen across the way from her and her friend.

Her hair flowed in waves from a loose ponytail that sat at the base of her neck and fell down the length of her back. The tank top she wore hugged her figure as if it were made for her and accentuated the toned muscles of her back. My gaze roamed lower, the definition of her legs was astounding. I was utterly entranced.

I caught sight of one of the men on the floor ogling her frame, no more than I had been just moments before. A growl nearly erupted from my throat, my muscles tensed as my body began to shake.

Dammit all.

Not here.

I clamped my jaw shut and inhaled through my nose as I calmed the beast within.

Not here.

The beast growled as it took in the poor excuse of a man.

"She is mine."

He began to claw his way out.

You cannot appear here!

"Mine."

She is not ours.

His growl rang in my ears. I shot the man a glare and narrowed my eyes. I was sure they had transformed into their slitted pits. The man's attention flicked to me. He paled; salty fear tinged the air from where he sat. The blood in his veins pumped into overdrive, his eyes widened.

Leave. Quietly. And quickly.

He shot up from his spot on the floor, gathered his things, and just short of sprinted out the door of the fitness center. He slipped on the growing snow and landed ass first on the pavement.

I smirked, the beast within now satisfied.

"Mine."

I rolled my eyes and wasted no time loading my warm up weights onto the bar ahead of me. I dipped below the worn metal bar and moved into my set. As I came up for my final rep, I caught the gaze of the entrancing woman's friend. She smiled and waved, the movement shook the entirety of her petite frame.

The beast purred within.

Looks as though we might meet her after all.

CHAPTER FOUR

Maeli

"*I find you enchanting, Maeli.*"

Alastor's little comment had been stuck in my head for the past week. He helped me clean up our spot and handed me his number before I grabbed my gym bag and left while he returned to his rack and finished his workout. I'd felt his molten gaze follow me as I walked out to my car in the fresh snow that had piled onto the cracked pavement.

"Fucking hell." I grunted as I lifted my oversized pile of books off of my little grey couch. I plopped them on the floor in front of my little bookcase I got off of a witch-ran furniture site. They specialized in spellbound furniture while keeping it discreet—which meant no boxes flying to my doorstep of their own accord.

"I'll put these away later."

It was less than two weeks before Christmas and most of these were going to be in boxes before then anyway. Orders had already begun to pile in.

I stood and stretched out the kinks in my back. I padded to my kitchen sink, flicked my wrist, and filled one of my plastic cups from the tap.

I stared at the filled cup, my mind wandered once more. *Should I text him?*

My phone buzzed in my pocket. I gulped my water down and pulled my phone out.

Hello Enchantress

My cup fell to the floor. My mouth went completely dry. It was Alastor.

CHAPTER FIVE

Maeli

How did you get my number?

I held my breath as three little dots popped up on my screen.

Your friend Kali gave it to me. I ran into her at the gym today.

Oh.

That's it. She's getting her coffee machine hacked.

I hope I'm not overstepping. I was beginning to think I'd never hear from you, Enchantress.

I mean...I wasn't necessarily avoiding the guy...just nerves.

I chewed my bottom lip.

> Maybe I was waiting. You know, build the suspense.

I tossed my phone on my cluttered counter. My heart pounded heavily in my chest.

Fuck. He's going to think I'm weird.

Flirting was never my strong suit. I left that to Kali, she was a master. If she had her eyes on someone she got them.

I on the other hand...my arsenal consisted of horribly dry jokes and dark humor with a sprinkle of out of context book references. And maybe a hex here and there if the guy pissed me off.

I'm just going to unsend it, I doubt he read my text yet.

My phone chose that moment to vibrate again.

It was him.

> Consider the suspense built.

I gulped as another message came through.

> May I have you for dinner?

My eyes nearly launched from my skull.

> My apologies, I mis-typed. I meant, may I take you to dinner?

I quickly tapped the keyboard on my screen, my stomach knotting.

I'm free tonight. As long as I'm not on the menu haha.

That, dear Maeli, is entirely up to you.

I'll pick you up at 7, Enchantress.

CHAPTER SIX

Maeli

I sent Alastor my address.

Then proceeded to panic and sprinted around my small one bedroom cottage like a madman.

I'd given up trying to clean by hand and swiftly flicked my wrists in every *witch* direction. Books flew from the floor and onto my shelf; scattered laundry was thrown into my top loading washer next to my kitchen. Blankets and pillows folded themselves before they slid into my hallway cupboard.

A mop slathered my wooden floors with lemon cleaner while I ran a rag across the now de-cluttered counter then sent all the dishes and trash to their respective spots.

I glanced at the clock above my stove.

5:45

I have a little over an hour until he gets here.

I snapped my fingertips and sent the mop, rags, and cleaner to put themselves away. The entire place was the cleanest it'd been in weeks.

I really should clean this way more often. Way easier.

My magic hummed in my veins.

I know, I need to put you to use more often.

It grumbled in agreement.

I beelined for my three piece bathroom and turned the shower all the way to scolding hot. My clothes fell to the ceramic tiled floor as I hopped under the running water. I squeezed my wintery-scented shampoo into my hand and lathered my hair before I rinsed and followed up with the matching conditioner.

Ten minutes later I rung my hair and wrapped myself in a towel; the room was filled with steam and soapy goodness.

I flipped on the fireplace in my bedroom as I walked in and dropped my towel as I headed for my closet.

Might be a small house but at least I have a walk-in closet. And a fireplace. Plus, it's mine.

I scoured my closet for anything that could pass for dinner. My options were slim to none considering most of my wardrobe consisted of various leggings, sweatpants, and T-shirts.

Maybe I should cancel.

I shook my head.

Dammit no. I'm doing this.

I dug around until I finally came up with a black, knee length dress with winged sleeves. I slipped it on and paired it with my only pair of heels. I glanced at the standing mirror next to my bed as I walked out and quickly tossed my hair into a curled ponytail. I swiped on a thin layer of makeup: shimmery eye shadow, blacked winged liner, mascara, and a deep red lip stain.

The bedside clock read 6:50. I darted out to the living room and snuck one last look in the bathroom mirror as I plucked my phone from the counter.

Welp, guess I'm really leaning into this whole 'Enchantress' thing.

I definitely look like a witch now.

Not that most humans would notice.

Gravel scattered as tires rolled down the unpaved driveway. I stepped outside and locked the door behind me. I subtly waved my fingers to set my wards in place as Alastor got out of his sleek metallic grey Lincoln.

Woah, fancy.

He held the front passenger door open as I neared.

The amber of his eyes heated and a breathtaking smile spread across his chiseled features. "You look ravishing, Maeli." He wore a full on three piece suit with his dress shirt hung open which provided me with a mouth watering view of his muscled chest that was perfectly accentuated with wisps of dark hair.

I licked my lips. "Speak for yourself, Alastor."

Oh my Gods. I did not just say that.

What is going on with me?

I slipped into the leather seat and he shut the door. I hungrily traced his every step until he got behind the wheel, a smirk played at the edge of his mouth.

And why am I okay with it?

"Ready, Enchantress?"

I nodded and we drove off.

Chapter Seven

Alastor

My breath caught.

The evening sky caressed her skin as it glowed in the moonlight. The jades of her eyes twinkled as she stepped from my car and grasped my extended hand. The dark fabric of her dress draped across her beautifully.

She smiled and the pounding in my chest skipped a beat, the beast within me for once in my long life...was utterly silent.

I closed the passenger door and dropped my keys into the palm of the attending valet. I followed closely, just a breath away. The small distance felt as if we were miles apart.

The click of her heels stopped on the pavement and her eyes widened. "We're eating...here?"

My brows furrowed.

Maybe she doesn't enjoy the style of cooking. I should've asked her what her preferences were before coming here.

"Is this not to your liking, Maeli?"

Her head snapped in my direction, the curls of her ponytail swished across her shoulders. "Are you kidding? This place is amazing! Holy shit."

I chuckled and released the tension that had spun its way into my shoulders.

"I'm glad to hear it. I take it you've been here before?"

"Years ago. My mo—" she paused. "An old teacher of mine brought me here after graduation. Best fucking meal of my life."

"Well, let's hope tonight's is even better"

She snorted. The sound brought a smile to my lips. "Yeah, no kidding. Anything would top that night."

"Oh?"

Maeli waved it off. "Let's just say that lady is permanently on my Do-Not-Contact list."

"Bad ex?" I asked, my jaw tensed.

We will destroy anyone who hurt her.

Patience, Beast.

CHAPTER EIGHT

Maeli

I gagged before bursting into a laughing fit. "Oh my Gods, no! That would be so wrong on so many levels."

Talk about a close knit coven. Gross.

"I've dated like three people total. And she was not one of them." Even though mother dearest was the reason they all ditched me in the first place...not that he needed to know that.

Fun, Maeli.

Not my-mom-is-a-crazy-witch bullshit.

Alastor guided me to the check-in stand occupied by a waiter that oozed pure boredom.

What are those things called?

I racked my brain and barely caught the guy's customer-service smile as it popped into place. Alastor said something to him and he motioned for us to follow.

"Maitre'd stand!" I smacked my fist into my palm.

"Maeli?" Alastor arched a brow with a question in his eyes.

Oh shit. I said that out loud.

Fucking hell.

"Sorry. I...uh...couldn't remember the name of the desk and it was bugging the hell out of me."

The corners of his eyes crinkled and a low laugh escaped from his lips as he pulled my chair out for me.

"Adorable."

I shot him a glare. "Do I look like a puppy?"

He smirked. The handsome son-of-a-bitch smirked. "Far from it, Maeli." I could've sworn his eyes darkened. "Personally, I'm more of a...cat person."

I choked. "Oh, is that so?"

"Absolutely. I find their company far more appealing."

Okay, so may-be I imagined the whole eyes-darkening thing.

Just an innocent comment.

"Cool. Cool. So, uh..."

Fucking hell, I'm drawing a blank.

Our waiter appeared which temporarily saved me from face-planting with my lack of conversation skills.

We ordered our food and Alastor added a bottle of wine to pair: medium rare steak with scalloped potatoes for me and a lobster tail with a rare filet and a side salad for him.

"How do you figure out if one wine tastes better with a steak than another?"

He sipped his water. "Truth be told, I have no idea. I find a favorite and typically stick with it. And it so happens that this was a recommendation from the head waiter the last time I was here."

My stomach twisted.

"...the last time I was here."

Maeli. No. You don't even know the guy. Play it cool.

Channel your inner Kali.

I forced myself to smirk and crossed my fingers it came off the way I wanted to. "Hmm...so do you bring all of your dates here, Alastor?" I quirked my brow as I poured our bottle of wine into my glass. I licked my lips and brought the red liquid to my mouth.

His gaze held mine, the corner of his mouth twitched.

Oh Gods.

Why? Why did I say that?

His pupils narrowed, the twitching of his lips morphed into a smirk. "Actually, you're the first I've brought here."

CHAPTER NINE

Maeli

Hours passed as we sat in the restaurant devouring our food and talking. And before we knew it, the staff were cleaning up and getting ready to close for the night.

Talking to Alastor—once I got past my whole lack of confidence and overthinking, and let's be honest, three overflowing glasses of wine—was easy. He had me laughing my ass off and I even pulled a chuckle or three out of him too.

He told me about his family or lack thereof. Alastor was an only child, just like me but he had no idea where his parents were—he'd been on his own since he was a kid. He'd moved to town just a few weeks ago and had initially planned on just passing through but his job required him to stay and so he decided to set up roots. Turns out, the behemoth of a man, was in the military until a year or two prior...and has a whole decade on me age wise.

Talk about aging like a fine wine.

We waited on the sidewalk outside for the valet to bring Alastor's car around. He wrapped his suit jacket around my shoulders, protecting me from the drop in temperature. I held it close, wrapping the fabric around me.

"Okay I did not plan on it being this cold out." I chattered as my body shivered.

"Well, Maeli, that does typically happen in the winter. Especially this close to the holiday." He chuckled and pulled me close into his side, the top of my head barely reached his chest.

Gods, this man is tall.

And warm as hell.

I snuggled into his heat, thankful that he seemed to be a walking furnace. "Aren't you cold?"

"Not even remotely. Not with you here, Enchantress."

Blood rushed to my cheeks, my stomach fluttered.

It's still pretty cold though.

I know another way we could warm up.

I blanched.

Holy shit, Maeli. Down girl.

Calm yourself.

I snuck a glance at Alastor as he watched the street, his gaze focused on the garage attached to the restaurant. My brows furrowed.

I didn't realize how close the parking was.

"They're sure taking their time. Do you think—"

Alastor's grip around my shoulders tightened and a low growl rumbled from his chest. My eyes widened.

He's...growling?

What man growls? This isn't some fantasy novel.

"Get behind me."

A knot formed in my stomach. "What? Why? Alastor what is going on?" I hissed.

Alarm bells rang in my ears. My magic sprinted to the surface, ready to pounce.

Heavy footsteps barreled down the concrete sidewalk. I peaked around Alastor to see several large men heading straight for us. I stepped behind Alastor and slipped my arms into the sleeves of his jacket so I'm not at a disadvantage. Tendrils of my magic weaved their way through my body and formed in the palms of my hands.

They aren't..they aren't human.

What the actual fuck is going on?

One of the men lunged forward a mere twenty feet from us.

His clothes ripped into shreds, scattered in the wind and the incoming flurries.

And in their place was a massive...wolf.

I blinked.

There aren't supposed to be any wolves around here.

My magic hummed and yanked me out of my stunned mind.

Fuck. He doesn't need to see any of this.

But...I needed to use my power...or we would've ended up being doggy kibble.

"Alastor, move!" I shoved my way in front of him and raised my hands. My magic flowed out of me and raced towards the fast approaching wolf shifter and his lackeys.

The wolf dodged it and aimed right for me.

Shit shit shit.

There was a loud rip behind me and a flash of black launched past me headfirst into the oncoming beast. It brought the wolf down in one swift move, tearing into its furry flesh and sending a large chunk of dark-grey fur flying through the cold winter air.

Three others howled as they shifted into their wolves. The blood lust was evident in their eyes even from where I stood.

Alastor.

Fuck he's probably flipping out.

The black form growled as it sped towards the other three wolves. I spun around, frantically searching for Alastor.

Where the hell did he go?

I mean not the best way to end a first date but don't tell me he bolted?

This is why I don't go on these things. Some bullshit always pops up.

He was nowhere to be found. I mentally kicked myself.

Too late now. At least he's probably safe.

I ran back to where the wolves were locked in their battle-of-the-beasts and tripped as I got closer.

"Godsdammit," I swore under my breath as pain pulsed around my ankle. I quickly glanced down and swirled my magic in my hand before sending it to heal my sprain.

Not the time for my clumsy ass.

Whatever jumped into the fray is going to get itself killed if I don't do something.

I jumped to my feet, thanked the Gods that the only heels I owned were easy to move in.

My arms swooped behind me as I sprinted towards them, magic surged through my veins. I shot my left hand forward, a bolt of golden electricity escaped from my palm. It hit the smallest of the remaining wolves square in its chest as it reared up on its hind legs. An ear splitting yelp echoed in the empty street as it fell to the ground with its eyes glazed over. Blood dribbled from its nose and sockets.

That's two down.

Two to go.

I chanced a quick look at the mystery creature and narrowed my eyes as it moved.

Dear Gods, that thing is fast.

It teared into another wolf and growled as a claw attached to the creature's massive black paw caught the wolf's eye and yanked it from its head.

Gross.

A deep growl sounded behind me. I turned, hot breath dampened the hair that barely remained in my ponytail.

The damned thing stared me down and smiled a mere inch or two from my face. A blood-chilling wolf's grin.

I fucking hate wolves.

I dropped to the ground as it snapped its jaws and rolled out of the way before launching back to my feet.

"Your breath stinks, Mutt."

Its eyes narrowed on me.

As it readied itself to lunge at me again, I swung my leg and kicked it directly in its side. The bone crunched, distracting the wolf. I jumped to the side as it howled in pain and launched myself onto it's back.

The wolf kicked below me, doing everything it could to buck me off.

I gripped its bronze fur in the palms of my hands and held on as it bounded through the street.

Definitely sticking to my rule of never riding a dog-boy.

These things are a damn pain.

And way too aggressive.

The wolf picked up speed as it raced towards one of the buildings lining the street.

"Oh you fucking, dumbass. Here I was going to give you a chance." I scoff.

The damned thing was going to ram itself into a thick ass wall to get rid of me.

I twisted the fur in my palms and yanked back while I channeled my power to boost my strength. It didn't work often but I could pack a serious punch for a few minutes here and there. Down side? The strength boost...I'd be on my ass for a week.

Oh well. Worth it.

The wolf pulled backwards, its footing failed and I went flying from its back as it slid paws up. I rolled onto the pavement and onto my feet.

The wolf was sprawled on the ground, its chest heaved.

I walked towards it, the heels of my shoes clicked on the ground. I clasped my hands behind my back and circled the barely conscious wolf. Another howl carried on the crisp winter breeze.

Guess this is the only one left.

I crouched down next to its massive head and rested my arms on the edges of my knees. I leaned forward and brought my lips close to its ear. "You know, I'm usually a nice and very understanding witch. But not when assholes like you go on a blood-fueled rampage." I let the ice fill my words as I whispered, "And it seems...you're the only one left. Do I let you go? Or show you some mercy and let you join the rest of your pack?"

Once the power that rushed through me calmed down, I was going to hate myself.

It always happened.

But right then, the magic within me ran the show, the last of my heart hidden with the strength pulled from just moments before.

When I let it consume me...I became like *her*. Like my bitch of a biological mother.

The wolf whimpered.

"Aw, is the little puppy going to beg? How cute."

Fucking hell.

Stop it.

Stop.

My magic roared in my ears, my pulse skyrocketed.

St—

A deep...almost velvety growl hummed from behind me. Slowly, I turned my head, my vision grew blurry. I blinked, my mind grew muddled. The ground raced towards me but before I fell into the imminent darkness I finally caught a glimpse of the creature.

A...panther?

CHAPTER TEN

Maeli

My head was pounding. Like some asshole took a jackhammer to my skull and set it to the max.

I groaned as I pulled my blanket up over my head and shielded myself from any light that trickled in.

Fucking hell.

What happened?

I rolled onto my back, my head still hidden under my down comforter and slowly blinked my eyes in the muted darkness.

How much did I drink last night?

Wait.

My blood stilled.

The memory of the night trampled through my head. The pain in my skull traveled the entire length of my body.

Every inch of me ached, inside and out. I squeezed my eyes shut, searching. My magic was nowhere to be found.

Son of a fucking bitch.

I bolted out of bed and hissed as the light from my hallway flooded my room.

My room.

But my wards...

I reached under my mattress and grabbed my knife. I squinted as I braced myself and padded to the door.

The urge to shout and ask who was there clawed at the back of my throat but I'd seen enough scary movies—and experienced enough of them first hand— to know better.

I crept down the small hallway, peaked around the corner, and scanned my kitchen first.

Empty.

I slid my narrowed gaze to the living room and there cuddled up on my couch fast asleep—clearly shirtless and snoring—was Alastor.

CHAPTER ELEVEN

Maeli

The acid in my stomach rose. It twisted and clawed as it made its way up through my esophagus. I darted into the bathroom and curled myself around the toilet as I hurled everything that was in my stomach.

My vision blurred, nothing but the taste and smell of bile filled my nose and mouth. Black spots flirted with the corners of my eyes as my head spun.

This is what I get for going on a date.

And letting my magic get the better of me.

"Maeli?" Groggy concern laced Alastor's voice from the door frame.

"Go away," I grumbled, head still stuck in the porcelain.

My mouth filled with saliva and I heaved again. My body began to shake.

A warm hand was at my back. I leaned into it as he drew circles on my pebbled flesh.

The nausea subsided and I rested my cheek on the cold seat, grateful I'd cleaned the day before. I groaned and slowly blinked as Alastor came into focus.

"What happened?'

His jaw ticked. "We had dinner and drank a bit too much wine so I brought you home and put you to bed." He flashed a tight lipped smile.

I pushed myself up to glare at him and immediately regretted it as another wave of nausea crashed into me. I laid my cheek back on the seat. "I'm not stupid, Alastor. I remember what happened."

His eyes narrowed. "Then why are you asking a question that you already know the answer to?" His face was rigid, stone cold. Even as he continued rubbing light circles into my skin.

"I mean—" I coughed, "You ditched me and ran off. What the hell happened with that and how did we end up back here? You shouldn't have been able to—"

Fuck.

"What all did you see, Alastor?"

He quirked a brow which broke his stoic expression. "I saw it all, Maeli. I was there the entire time."

I huffed. "Dude. I'm not stupid. I turned around and you vanished. I went looking and you were nowhere to be found. I don't expect a human to just be okay and handle this shit like a champ but I'm not a freaking idiot. Don't lie to me. You hightailed it—"

Hold on a minute.

—a low growl rumbled from his chest.

There was a loud rip behind me and a flash of black launched past me...

"No." I shook my head. "No there's no fucking way."

"Maeli..."

I shot up and the words fell from my lips, "You're a fucking *panther-shifter*? Are you shitting me?"

"I can explain." Alastor rushed out as he grabbed my shoulders to keep the dizziness from knocking my stunned ass to the ground.

"Damn right you can explain."

He saw what I am.

The moment I said yes, I signed my death sentence. And I didn't even know it.

Wolves were one thing.

But panthers?

Our species killed each other. Granted...witches started it but the fact still remained.

This guy—this *panther*—was going to kill me.

If I didn't kill him first.

Chapter Twelve

Maeli

"What's your deal, Alastor?" I panted as sweat beads dripped down my forehead and caused tangled strands of my hair to stick to my skin.

I'd stood and tried to bolt out of my bathroom only to collapse the moment I was vertical and he'd caught me before I could crack my head on the floor. Alastor then took it upon himself to carry me to my couch. I was fuming.

He sat on the fluffy maroon rug in the center of my living room, his long toned legs sprawled out in front of him. His brows furrowed. "What do you mean?"

So he's going to play dumb. Great.

"Dude, come on. I'm completely fried. Don't do this and play dumb. Why am I still alive?" I shook my head, what little energy I had quickly draining, and leaned back into the cushions.

If I have to deal with this bullshit, I'm at least going to be comfortable.

"Maeli, you're still alive because you stood your ground against those canines. It was quite awe inspiring actually."

I scoffed. "Of course I can handle my own, jackass. I'm not talking about the damn mutts. Why didn't you kill me? I collapsed. My powers literally ditched my body and said 'see ya later'."

Is he dense?

My gaze flicked towards him. The guy was still completely shirtless, every inch of toned muscle including the delicious six-pack defined on his stomach, was on full display.

Dense.

And hot.

I sighed.

At least my death will be at the paws of some serious eye candy.

My headache pounded at the base of my skull, threatening to come back with a vengeance. I squeezed my eyes shut and draped my arm over to further block out the light in the room.

The rug shifted on the floor.

Here we go.

Please make it swift.

The cushions on the far end of the couch near my feet sunk in under Alastor's weight.

Not exactly the best angle to gut someone but okay.

Warmth flooded my skin as he placed his palm on the heel of my foot, his thumbs rubbed the padded flesh below my toes.

"Massage before death? Weird." I mumbled.

"Why are you convinced I'd want to or even be able to kill you, Maeli?" Hurt pressed into each word as he spoke.

"Because of what we are? It's kind of ingrained in the whole panther gene." I grunted as he pressed further into the tender tissue and slowly moved to my ankle. I sighed as he rubbed the spot I'd sprained. I healed it but I'd still be a bit sore for a while.

His voice deepened, "Dear, I am not like others of my kind. I see no reason to harm someone without valid reason. Especially someone as *enchanting* as you." Heat rushed to my cheeks, my stomach twisted.

Enchanting.

Enchantress.

"Wait a damned minute. Did you know what I was the whole ass time?" I bolted upright as I shouted and instantly regretted it as the throbbing behind my eyes ramped up. I moaned from the pain and flopped back down.

"I had a feeling," he chuckled. "You need to rest, you know. Bouncing around, as adorable as it is, is going to do nothing but increase your recovery time."

His hands moved up my legs as he continued to massage every sore inch of me.

"And before you ask, I've worked with a few witches in the past. I'm well aware of the wear and tear magic can have on your body, even if it's not from personal experience. I've seen enough throughout my years."

I groaned as he pressed into a particularly sensitive spot. "You act like you're older than you are."

He snickered. "Well, my dear Maeli, that's because I am."

"Of course you are," I snipped, my heart not completely in it. "So spill, what's the real number, Old Man?"

"Pardon me, Miss Maeli, I may be old to you, however, I am still young for my species. I'm just shy of my 200th birthday. Sticking to being in my late thirties or early forties just simplifies things. As I'm sure you know."

Ain't that the truth.

I couldn't count the amount of times I had to explain why certain things happened around me—plates would randomly fly across a room, sudden drop in temperature inside a heated building, break a leg and then it would miraculously heal a day or two later. That one had been the hardest. And exactly how Kali found out what I was. My mother had nearly killed me for it, even though she was the very reason my leg had broken...along with a few ribs.

Not too long after that I'd cut ties with her and moved across town and into the little cottage I called home. Heavy wards and all. As far as I was concerned, she thought I'd left town. Not a word from her since.

I pulled myself from my runaway thoughts. "Okay, so you've got a couple centuries under your belt. What else are you hiding, Kitty-cat?"

He grinned and my heart pounded in my chest. "I'm an open book at this point. Ask away."

"Parents?"

"Truly don't know where they reside. We have rather...different views on things." He clipped as his jaw tensed.

"Fair enough. Alright. You mentioned the military. What did you *actually* do? Last I recalled, supernaturals weren't allowed in."

He smirked. "Typically. However, there are certain *lesser known* sectors which rely on our...talents if you will. I worked for a private sector. Still do in a sense. Which was what brought me here."

I blinked.

So, it wasn't all a lie.

Cool.

He continued, "The wolves we encountered last night, that wasn't the first instance around here. There's been several reports of animal attacks in the area. Obviously authorities reported bears and other animals that are easy to write off in a small town surrounded by mountains and an abundant forest. Especially given the individuals whom we believe to be orchestrating the attacks."

My eyes widened. I'd heard of the attacks but didn't think anything of it. Alastor was right—it really was the perfect place for it. "Who do you think it is?"

His lips pressed into a thin line. "We have a few suspects but they're tricky and have flown under the radar."

"Fuck."

"Yeah."

I chewed the inside of my mouth. "Is there any way I can help? I have friends here that I don't want to see hurt."

Okay, one friend, but still.

Kali was a social butterfly but when we weren't together, we both kinda did our own thing. Main difference, she actually went outside more often. Whereas my activities consisted of the bookstore, the gym, lunch dates with Kali, and work. Which I did from home.

Shit.

Work.

"Do you know where my phone is?" Panic raced through me. "Fuck. Fuck. Fuck." I tried sitting up but Alastor gently pushed me down.

"I'm sure it's around here somewhere. When was the last time you had it?" He grabbed a throw blanket off the back of my couch and draped it over me, padding the fabric as he stood.

I racked my brain trying to remember. "I think I took it with me last night but I didn't check it once I left the house. Maybe it's in my purse?" I pinched the bridge of my nose.

"I'll check. I brought your purse in when I carried you home. Do you mind if I search through it or would you rather me bring it to you?"

"Just bring it to me please," I breathed. "How did you get us in anyhow? My wards should've stayed intact even with my magic depleted."

"I know my way around a few witch wards—even one's as strong as yours, Maeli." He shrugged and flashed another grin. "Quite the powerful little witch, aren't you?"

I shot him a glare as heat returned to the apples of my cheeks. "Well, I have a lot of time to practice."

The toe curling laughter echoed down the hall as he walked to my room.

No hesitation.

Kinda creepy.

But it's also...kinda hot.

Only a few minutes passed until he strode back out to my living room with my little emerald green bag in tow. The second he reached his arm out to give it to me, I snatched my purse and dug through it like a mad man.

Finally.

I let out a sigh of relief when I found my phone tucked in one of the small inner pockets.

The screen won't light up.

*It was at full charge when he picked me up for dinner.
What gives?*

I reached around the side of my couch and pulled out a
charge cord—one of the many I stashed around the cottage.

It only took a minute or two for my screen to flash to life.

I did a double take.

There's no way. That can't be right

"Uh, Alastor, how long was I out for?"

"It's been a few days, close to a week. Why?"

Notifications flooded my screen as my service kicked in.
Order after order.

Panic pierced into me. My heart beat pummeled in my
chest. My throat constricted; air was unable to reach my
lungs.

Fuck. Fuck. How am I going to get these out?

A whole ass week.

My shop. Fucking shit.

Black spots fluttered in the outer rings of my vision as
salty tears dripped from my lashes. Sweat rapidly reap-
peared and my palms grew clammy.

"Maeli!"

What do I do?

A week away from my business.

I'm going to be in the shitter.

How am I going to fix this?

Warm lips smashed against mine and pulled me from my
downward spiral. "Ala—" He pressed further and deep-

ened the kiss. Something stirred in the pit of my stomach. I slipped my tongue between us as I licked his lips and pulled his bottom lip between my teeth and nipped lightly. A growl rose from his chest.

His large calloused hands gently grabbed my shoulders as his thumbs circled the rounded tops before he pulled back and released me.

I moaned in protest and he chuckled softly. "You okay?"

My heart is pounding and the hottest guy I've ever seen just laid one of the juiciest kisses I've had in ages on me.

"I don't know," I sighed. Exhaustion crashed over me.

Alastor brushed a strand of hair from my eyes while his concerned gaze searched mine. "Does that happen often? Panic attacks?"

I turned my head, my gaze dropped and focused on the little wisps of fluff on my rug. I closed in on myself and my shoulders sagged forward.

I was worried about this man killing me less than an hour ago.

And now I just...

Alastor took my chin between his thumb and forefinger as he turned me to face him again. "Hey," he said softly. "Look at me, Maeli." I dragged my unfocused gaze upward and glanced at him from beneath my lashes. He tilted my chin so I had to look directly into the molten depths of his softened eyes.

"You experiencing that...I'm not going to say it's normal because not everyone deals with them...but having them doesn't make you any less of a person. It doesn't make you weak. It's something you experience. And...that's okay."

Tears pooled as a lump lodged in my throat.

"We've only just begun to know each other but please don't hide from me. I'm here for you, if you'll allow me." That did it.

A sob broke from within me.

Alastor pulled me into his arms as he cradled me while the turmoil from the wolf ran in. My magic was fully depleted. The fact that I'd disappeared off the face of the planet for almost a week and my online business might have plummeted because of it, crashed over me in waves.

Chapter Thirteen

Maeli

He held me for what felt like hours.

Once the tears stopped flowing, I gulped down some water Alastor had grabbed for me and I finally pulled it together. After I sorted through all the online orders that had piled up while I was unconscious, I swallowed my pride—and the guilt—and asked Alastor to help, if he had the time.

"Anything you need, Maeli. I'm all yours."

I padded to my room and grabbed my laptop from beneath my bed. I loaded the admin page for my shop and it was already overloaded with backorders. I pointed around the living room at things for Alastor to grab and showed him how to package everything: wrap the books individually, tuck the stickers and artwork into the flaps of the wrapping, how to fold the clothing to fit, and which freebies to include.

I printed off shipping labels and folded the boxes to ship as we went. Then stuffed the tops and bottoms of each package with crinkled paper to add extra padding.

"Here I thought all the books on your back wall were a part of your personal collection. How long have you owned your shop?"

"Just shy of a year. I have a few author friends and wanted to support them and since we love reading I figured I might as well open a store. They were the first ones I stocked. Most of these are signed." I reached across the counter for my water. "As for my personal collection…unfortunately until my magic recharges I can't get to them. They're in my library downstairs. Which, as you can probably guess, I have under a major protection spell and it's only accessible by a little portal enchantment I made a while ago."

He nodded as a smile graced his sharp features. "How interesting. I take it since you have very limited photos spread throughout your home, all of which include Kali, that she is one of your author friends?"

"Yeap. And a great one too." I smiled up at his towering figure. "She has over thirty books published across a ton of different genres. I don't know how she does it."

He held up one of the small paperbacks, a paranormal romance.

Well, isn't this ironic?

"Is this one of her works by chance?" He flipped it over and skimmed the blurb on the back.

"Yeah, it's actually one of her new ones. It's about pirates and sirens."

"I might have to give this a read. Do you mind?"

"Sure, go for it but I'm going to warn you, it is a romance novel."

His eyes flashed to mine, heat radiated from within them. A smirk teased the corner of his lips and my gaze flicked to them, licking my own. "Romance novels happen to be a favorite of mine."

"Oh really?" I bit my lip and glanced up from beneath my lashes. "They happen to be a favorite of mine, too."

"Something else we have in common then." Alastor leaned closer to me, the huskiness of his voice sent chills down my spine.

"Mhm." I barely mustered as my breath hitched.

He ran his fingers through my hair as he slowly brought his face closer to mine. My eyes slid closed as I tilted my chin.

"Maeli..." he moaned, his breath warm on my lips.

I reached up and wrapped my arms around his neck to close the distance as I crashed my mouth against his.

CHAPTER FOURTEEN

Maeli

Heat rushed to my center as our kiss deepened. My stomach twisted with each heavy breath between us. My nails dug into his back as his plump lips slowly explored the pink flesh along my jaw.

A moan slipped from my mouth as Alastor licked and sucked his way down my exposed neck. His hands roamed over the sensitive skin above the waistband of my pants. "Oh Gods."

He slipped his fingers under the fabric of my shirt and pressed the tips into my skin as he inched higher and higher. I sucked in a breath as the pads of his thumbs brushed just below my breasts.

"Is..is this okay, Maeli?" He rasped. His head was still bent as he nestled in against my collarbone.

I nipped his ear as I murmured my answer. He let out a growl and hoisted me on to the counter while he gripped my ass. The packing supplies and books scattered to the floor. I ran my hands down the planes of his chest and twirled my fingers in the dark wisps spread across the never ending muscles. I traced the trail that led to the hem of his sweatpants and ran the tip of my finger along his skin.

He let out a groan as I moved my lips and nipped his beautifully dark skin as I went. His body began to hum, almost vibrating as I closed in just inches above the waistband of his pants.

I pulled back and flashed a smirk before I yanked his head down to mine. Our lips clashed, our tongues swirled around one another in need. I wrapped my legs around his waist, my center flush with his very hard and thick member.

Thank the Gods I have tall counters.

Alastor reached around as he regained his grip on my ass and thrusted my center against his hard cock. I let out a moan, my body needed more. I ground against him as he gripped me harder. He released one hand from my hungry body and slid his thick fingers under my top. I moaned into him as he pinched and squeezed my nipples.

"Off. Now." I panted, my body on fire.

He tore the thin fabric from my body and flung it to the side, his mouth quickly found the pebbled peaks and began to feast heavily. His tongue swirled and sucked at each nipple as his teeth grazed my tender flesh. My blood pulsed through my veins and heated with every stroke of his tongue.

Hints of my magic stirred within me and slowly came back to life.

Oh your timing couldn't be better.

I bit into Alastor's shoulder and he let out a muffled groan. His body shook against me.

My magic simmered at the surface while my strength grew as each moment passed.

I purred his name and immediately caught his attention. His head shot up, his eyes slitted and widened as they took in the smirk plastered on my face.

I pulled him close and whispered into his ear, "Have you used a safe word before, Alastor?"

His tongue licked my shoulder as he nodded. A shiver echoed down my spine.

Chapter Fifteen

Maeli

I flicked my wrist and summoned some of my toys from my bedroom as I pulled Alastor to the couch and pushed him back onto the cushions. He landed with a thud and a curious smirk, his eyes twinkled in the fluorescents. I swirled my fingers in the air to dim the lights around us.

"Arms up, pretty boy," I purred as one of my ropes tied itself around his wrists before anchoring to the hooks I had hidden in the wall. My black leather flogger floated to me, the hilt rested in the palm of my hand. "Ready for some fun...Alastor?" My tongue flicked across my bottom lip as I drew out his name, relishing the taste of it on my tongue.

He nodded, hunger heavy in his eyes and on the brink of escape.

I stepped forward and straddled his lap as I ran the leather straps along his skin. Alastor shivered as he pulled his bottom lip between his teeth, a growl began to build within his chest. He wriggled beneath me. I snapped my fingers and latched his ankles to the floor by another set of straps carefully hidden then turned on my heel so that my back faced him.

Music played quietly from my stereo as I started to swish my hips. I grasped Alastor's thighs and slowly lowered myself in front of him, grinding my ass in his lap. His hard member was ready to burst through his sweats as I leaned forward and slowly inched myself down until I could grab my ankles. He groaned as I waggled my hips in front of him.

I danced and teased him until he was ready to burst while beads of sweat ran down his chest. Once he was ready, I gently pulled a blind fold over his eyes. He whimpered and I kissed along his thick neck. I nipped as I moved lower and mirrored his movements from earlier then teasingly licked along his collarbone.

"Please...Maeli," he rasped.

"Maeli? Hmm, I thought you had another name for me, Alastor." I flicked his nipple with my tongue.

He let out a ragged breath. "Please...Enchantress." His cock twitched through his sweats. My mouth watered; the need to taste his large member pulsed through me. My magic rumbled in the pit of my stomach, hungry.

Still weird. It never reacts to someone like this.

I got on my knees, my body reached across his as I ran my fingers along the trail of wispy dark hair to his waistband once more. I slipped the tips beneath the hem and slowly drew circles along his sensitive skin before I pulled the fabric down over his hips and dropped them to his ankles, adding to the restraints.

The bulge in his boxers was on the brink of tearing through. I yanked them away, his rock hard cock sprung forward.

Holy shit.

It was larger than I imagined; easily a full 12 inches in length. I leaned forward and licked the head, a bead of pre-cum glistened at the top.

"Fuck," he growled.

I glanced up as I dragged my tongue up his length. Every muscle of his twitched and strained. A grin spread across my cheeks as excitement bubbled below the surface.

My lips closed around him as I took as much of him as I could into my mouth, the head of his cock hit the back of my throat as I swallowed him. His hips bucked below me as I ran my tongue along his shaft and sucked as I bobbed up and down. I cupped his balls in the palm of my hand and fondled them between my fingers. I gave a light squeeze. He let out another grunt then thrusted himself deeper.

I gagged with the movement, my eyes watered.

"Fuck, I'm sorry, Maeli." Rope and leather tear as he broke free from the restraints. His arms wrapped around me as he picked me up and lifted me onto his lap. He tilted my chin up so that he was able to see clearly into my tear filled eyes. "I'm sorry, I lost control. Are you okay?" He rushed, worry creased across his forehead.

I was gobsmacked, my eyes wide and a bit confused. "Yeah, I'm fine," I stuttered, taken back by his reaction.

"Are you sure? I didn't hurt you?" His brows furrowed deeper, pain laced the rough velvet of his voice.

I wiggled in his grasp and adjusted so my thighs fell on either side of him, his member pressed between us. I glanced down, admiring the hardness between us before I switched my focus back to his face and glanced from below my lashes. "You didn't hurt me, Alastor." I licked my lips. "I actually...really enjoyed it...I want to see you lose control," I rasped and leaned forward. "I want to see that beast inside of you. Let it out and take me."

CHAPTER SIXTEEN

Alastor

"I want to see that beast inside of you. Let it out and take me."

My heart nearly stopped. The beast within me, stunned.

She wants both of us.

Doubt pricked at the nape of my neck.

Show her.

Show her how much we want her. How much we need her.

Her eyes locked with mine, the depths swirled within them, a longing—a hunger. It was only the beginning. And she had no idea. Not yet.

I searched her gaze as guilt washed over me. I couldn't tell her the truth as of yet. It was far too soon. "Do you trust me, Enchantress?"

She nodded as she nibbled on her bottom lip.

As I stood with her still clutched to my chest, she wrapped her thighs around my waist and my cock slid against her center. She shook at the contact, a muffled moan fell from her beautiful lips as she pressed her head against my chest. I nestled my face in her hair atop her head and breathed in her intoxicating scent as I carried her to her bedroom.

I gently laid her back on the plush mattress, Her beautifully strong, curved body surrounded by pillows. I blew a haughty trail along her skin, her nipples pebbling at the air as it caressed her breasts.

"Stay here for but a moment, Enchantress." I purred as I kissed the spot just below her navel.

She squirmed and pressed her thighs together. A wave of her sweet arousal rushed over me, my cock twitched in response, my hardness almost painful. She fluttered her lidded gaze, her need dripped from each syllable as she spoke, "What if I don't want to?" She traced her delicate fingers under her tender breasts before she slowly edged towards her abdomen. I let out a growl as she neared the v between her hips.

I dashed forward and wrapped my hand around her wrist just before she reached her folds, visibly slick with her ne ed."Now, Enchantress. Don't misbehave," I breathed, the heat caressed her sensitive skin. "Be a good girl and stay here, dearest."

She whimpered as I stepped away, her chest heaved. I turned on my heel, taking my time as I grabbed her box of tricks she'd flown into the living room. I quickly skimmed the remaining contents.

Perfect.

As I entered my Enchantress's bedroom once more, my breath caught. Little moans escaped from between her lips as her breasts heaved from her rapid breathing. Her fingers swirled around her pink mound between her thighs. Her eyes slipped closed and her mouth formed a perfect o as she spread her thighs and provided me with a perfect view.

I stalked up to where she laid hot and panting on her bed. As I crawled onto the blanketed mattress, my weight pressed onto the unbelievably soft duvet. I settled myself between her thighs, pressing them further apart as she continued her ministrations. She groaned as the pressure built within her. The rhythm of her heart pounded in her chest as blood pumped through her veins, her body heat rose as she neared her climax.

Just before her pleasure washed over her, I grasped her wrist, gently pulled it away, and braced both of her hands above her head. I leaned down and whispered into the crook of her neck, "Trying to have some fun without me, Enchantress? Seems as though someone doesn't know how to behave." I licked the soft flesh then nipped and sucked it between my teeth. She gasped as I left my mark.

My Enchantress wriggled beneath me, no doubt she was searching for any form of friction to alleviate the coiled tension within her. I pulled a pair of cuffs from her collection and with one free hand I clasped them around her wrists. Once she was secured, I grabbed another bundle of black rope, thrilled to find that I hadn't torn through the only ones she possessed during our little escapade in the living room.

I quickly slipped the rope through the metal on her handcuffs and secured them to her headrest. My hunger pulsed through my veins as my gaze roamed her perfect taut body; her nipples erect at the center of her soft breasts that fit perfectly in the palm of my hands, the softness of her stomach and the nectar filled valley between her hips. Her luscious, thick thighs begging to be stroked.

I ran my tongue along my lips which caused her to whimper under my gaze.

"Please, Alastor. Please," she panted. "I need you."

My cock twitched at her words. I gripped the head in my hand and pumped myself through my tight grip down to the base. "You need me, Enchantress? Show me. Beg for it." I demanded as I dragged out another stroke along my painfully hard length.

She sucked in a breath, her thighs squirmed under my scrutiny. "Please. I need you. I neeed you inside me. Please!"

I crawled closer, my dick still firmly grasped within my palm. My thighs ghosted against her flushed skin. I tipped my head towards her center and rubbed it against her clit. Her hips bucked at the contact.

I rubbed my head against her again, this time I slowly continued the motion. Her hips rocked with each gentle thrust. "More...please. I–" She rasped. "I need more."

I pulled back, her eyes pleaded and I smacked myself against the bundle of nerves. She let out a squeak, the rosiness of her cheeks deepened. I reached between us and began thumbing her clit as I stroked two fingers along her folds. Her pants grew ragged with each swipe along her entrance. I increased the pace and continued to rub her mound with my thumb, I plunged my fingers into her heat. I thrusted in and out then added a third, readying her for my length. Her hips rocked against my hand and she reached her peak.

I smirked as I leaned over her body, our eyes locked. "Come for me, Enchantress. I want to hear you scream my name."

Her mouth fell open as I latched my lips onto her rosy peak. My tongue lapped the bud as I stroked her through her orgasm, her body heaved beneath me.

"Fuck," she moaned. "Al-" Thrust. "Alastor-" Another thrust then I pinched her nipple between my teeth as my thumb pressed harder against her clit. "I'm coming!" A scream ripped from her as she melted on my fingers, my name softly fell from her lips.

"Such a good girl," I groaned.

I slid my fingers from her wet heat and inhaled her sweet scent as I brought them to my lips. Her eyes fluttered open and locked with mine as I sucked her juices from the tips of my fingers.

"A Good Girl deserves a special reward, don't you think, Maeli?"

Her head bobbed as she nodded excitedly. The action pulled a low chuckle from my throat.

Such an adorable Enchantress.

I thrust my hips forward. My dick slowly glided along her center as I brushed against her clit. She let out another little moan and I pulled back. I grasped my length and angled myself at her entrance then guided the tip in.

Inch by inch I glided painstakingly slow into her slick warmth. She pulsed around my shaft as I pushed my cock deeper between her folds.

I moaned, fully sheathed inside her walls. "You take me so well, don't you?"

I thrusted my hips, our bodies flush against one another before I pulled out all the way to the hilt and rammed back into her depths.

She moaned with each thrust. Her body clenched around me as I rode her through another wave of pleasure, her center pulsed around me. I took her lips with mine as I pushed into her again, our hunger unsated. I need more of her. *We* need more of her.

My palms massaged her soft breasts. I tweaked her pert nipples as I continued to pound into her. My head hit her cervix as I increased our pace. I growled as she pulled my lip between her teeth and bit to the point of drawing blood. She licked the droplets from my lip, as our hunger chased one another. I growled as she pulled my tongue and sucked on it as her hips rushed to meet mine.

"Absolutely *perfect,*" I groaned as I felt her clench around my shaft.

"Come with me, Enchantress. I want to be your undoing."

Over movements became fevered. We thrusted against one another as we neared our joined climax. I snaked my fingers through her hair and held her lips against mine as I pounded into her. A roar ripped from my chest just as she screamed out and clenched around my cock as her orgasm crashed over her.

I fell and laid beside her breathless body. I wrapped my arms around her and pulled her against me.

I brushed her hair to the side. "You're absolutely breathtaking, Maeli," I murmured as I placed a light kiss along the side of her neck.

She mumbled something in return, too low for even my heightened hearing to catch and drifted off to sleep in my arms.

My heart pounded.

Sleep well, My heart.

And know...at all costs, I shall protect you.

Chapter Seventeen

Maeli

It had been a hell of a long time since I'd gotten my hands on a guy and, my Gods, Alastor had not disappointed. I'd fallen asleep within minutes and didn't wake again until the following morning.

Another day had been lost and I woke up in a panic. I had two days until Christmas and was out of time. I sprinted from my room as my heart pounded in my chest.

I stopped mid stride.

Alastor sat at the kitchen counter, coffee in hand and a second one next to him. He peered over the rim of his mug.

Your mug, Maeli. Not his.

Could be his...

Stop it.

I shook my head to clear the runaway thought. "What are you still doing here?" I glanced around the kitchen and stopped in front of him, reached over the counter top to grab the second coffee—I fully assumed it was for me.

"I'm not one to simply run out after having a bit of fun, Maeli," I took another sip. "Besides, you seemed as though you might need some more rest." He smirked.

My cheeks flushed. "Well. Thanks, I guess." I peered into the living room. "Where did everything go? I had a mountain to get through yesterday..."

He shrugged and checked his watch.

Since when did he have a watch on?

"I had some spare time after I checked up on the case I'm working on. I thought I'd lighten the load."

I gaped at him. "I...Thank you. You didn't have to do that."

"Maybe not, however, as I said, I had the spare time." He glanced at his watch again and I furrowed my brows.

"Do you need to be somewhere?" I pointed at his wrist. "You keep checking that thing."

He let out a sigh and my heart deflated. "Unfortunately yes. I have an appointment with a potential informant."

I pouted. "Oh, okay."

Alastor stood and circled the counter then rinsed his mug in the sink before he set it to the side.

I guess he'll be back?

He strode to where I leaned against the counter and placed a peck on top of my head. "I'll be back. I've rather enjoyed our...time together." His fingers pressed into my upper back.

And it occurred to me that in my rush to get out here...

I was still buck-ass naked.

Blood rushed to my face as I glanced up at him in horror.

He chuckled and placed a quick kiss on my lips before he headed for the front door. His sudden absence left me flustered and I ached for more.

Realization dawned on me.

We knew almost nothing about each other.

Why is he sticking around here, in my *house?*

My magic rumbled in my stomach mirroring a laugh.

Okay, I'm not complaining...but it's weird.

CHAPTER EIGHTEEN

Maeli

Alastor ended up coming back briefly later that night with a bouquet of flowers in tow. We'd relaxed at my cottage and flipped through raunchy holiday movies and a few classics as we stayed up late into the night. He'd brought dinner and I provided the hot cocoa and popcorn afterwards.

We talked deep into the night and as the sun began to rise the next morning...he was deep into me. Our moans filled the small cottage into the late morning and again that evening. The days were going by way too fast.

Alastor left but promised to return the following day. Christmas day.

It'd be the first time since I was still in contact with my witch of a mother, that I wouldn't be spending the holiday alone.

Damned if I actually let the bubble of excitement fuel me that morning.

I bounced around the house having woken at the brink of dawn; cleaned, baked and wrapped a story favorite of mine that I felt Alastor would enjoy. After spending a few days together, it seemed as though we had a lot of similar interests including the type of books we gravitated towards. We'd even spent an hour or two the day before just enjoying each other's presence while we read in silence. It had been pure bliss.

I flew around the kitchen as I put my finishing touches on the food I had planned for us later in the day. A meat-lovers lasagna, a loaf of garlic bread—both made entirely from scratch—and a simple garden salad. Dessert wise, I had a fresh apple pie in the oven and a little lacey gift stashed in my closet. I double checked the time left for the pie and darted to my bathroom for a quick shower before getting dressed. Alastor was due within the hour.

I slipped on the black lingerie I rush ordered when I realized he would be at my cottage again. I wanted to give him another little gift we could enjoy together. I snorted when I twirled in front of my mirror and slipped on a pair of leggings and a loose v-neck before tossing my hair into another ponytail. I snickered as I remembered the way he'd gripped it the day before as he pounded into me from behind.

Who knew I'd be having some panther—a hot one who didn't want to end my small existence—in my bed and chowing down on my food?

Definitely not me.

I skipped into the kitchen then pulled the pie from the oven as it beeped and set it on the stove; I hummed softly as I did so.

I sliced a knife into the center once it cooled to divide it into eighths when a knock sounded at my front door.

I shouted over my shoulder, "Come in!"

I finished slicing and there was no sound, no click of the door unlocking.

Maybe he didn't hear me.

I walked towards my front door and unlocked it, pulling the heavy wood open. And there on my footstep..was a fucking wolf. A huge ass wolf, with pure hate in its bright blue eyes.

I groaned. Irritation flowed through me as my magic roared in my ears. This was not how I wanted to spend my holiday.

Merry Fucking Shiftmas to me.

Epilogue

The Smutacular Adventures of Witches and Shifters

Book One

End

Also by S. P. Icey

Suck Me Harder: A Smutty Vampire Romance (June 2024)

Have A Holly Jolly Shiftmas: A Smutacular Witchy Shifter
Novella (December 2024)

Novella Number Three (Title to be announce) (2025)

Social Media

Instagram: @author.s.p.icey

Facebook: Author S. P. Icey

Signed Books and Merch:

https://snowpirebooksllc.myshopify.com/